DOG DIARIES

SPARKY

DOG DIARIES

#1: GINGER
A puppy-mill survivor in search of a *furever* family

#2: BUDDY
The first Seeing Eye guide dog

#3: BARRY
Legendary rescue dog of the Great Saint Bernard Hospice

#4: TOGO
Unsung hero of the 1925 Nome Serum Run

#5: DASH
One of two dogs to travel to the New World aboard the *Mayflower*

#6: SWEETIE
George Washington's "perfect" foxhound

#7: STUBBY
One of the greatest dogs in military history

#8: FALA
"Assistant" to President Franklin Delano Roosevelt

#9: SPARKY
Fire dog veteran of the Great Chicago Fire

SPECIAL CROSSOVER EDITION

DOG DIARIES

SPARKY

BY KATE KLIMO • ILLUSTRATED BY TIM JESSELL

RANDOM HOUSE 🏠 NEW YORK

The author and editor would like to thank Russell Lewis, executive vice president and chief historian at Chicago History Museum, for his assistance in the preparation of this book.

Text copyright © 2016 by Kate Klimo
Cover art and interior illustrations copyright © 2016 by Tim Jessell
Photographs courtesy of Chicago History Museum, pp. ix, 147; York County Heritage Trust, York, PA, p. 148; Skokie Heritage Museum, p. 149 (top); © Seth Casteel, p. 149 (bottom)

Visit us on the Web! randomhousekids.com

Educators and librarians, for a variety of teaching tools, visit us at RHTeachersLibrarians.com

Library of Congress Cataloging-in-Publication Data
Names: Klimo, Kate, author. | Jessell, Tim, illustrator.
Title: Sparky / by Kate Klimo ; illustrated by Tim Jessell.
Description: First edition. | New York : Random House, [2016] | Series: Dog diaries ; 9 |
Summary: "A firedog from the Maxwell Street fire station tells the story of the Great Chicago Fire" —Provided by publisher.
Identifiers: LCCN 2015021317 | ISBN 978-0-553-53493-1 (trade) |
ISBN 978-0-553-53494-8 (lib. bdg.) |
ISBN 978-0-553-53495-5 (ebook)
Subjects: LCSH: Dalmatian dog—Juvenile fiction. | Great Fire, Chicago, Ill., 1871—Juvenile fiction. | CYAC: Dalmatian dog—Fiction. | Dogs—Fiction. | Fire fighters—Fiction. | Great Fire, Chicago, Ill., 1871—Fiction. | Chicago (Ill.)—History—To 1875—Fiction.
Classification: LCC PZ10.3.K686 Sp 2016 | DDC [Fic]—dc23

Printed in the United States of America

10 9 8 7 6 5 4 3 2 1

First Edition

To the Michael Ryan in my life,
a hero if ever there was one
—K.K.

For the two- and four-legged who show
inspiring courage under fire
—T.J.

Author's Note

There really was a fire station on Maxwell Street. It was the home of the *Little Giant,* among the city's first steam engines and the first rig to show up at the scene of the Great Fire. The characters in this story—dog, horse, and human—are figments of this author's imagination.

CONTENTS

LITTLE GIANT No. 6, 1874

That's me!

The real members of Engine Company 6 pose with the *Little Giant,* three years after the Great Fire.

THE KEEPER

The lads at the fire station named me Sparky. I come from a time, over one hundred years ago, when it was horses, not motorized engines, that hauled equipment to the scene of a fire. Back then, firemen depended on dogs to keep their horses calm and obedient. In those grand old days, before Dalmatians became little more than station mascots, it really *meant* something to be a fire dog. And I was one of the best.

Fires were breaking out all over the South Side of Chicago on the winter's eve in 1867 when my mum whelped beneath the stairs of the Maxwell Street station. There were eleven of us: Plug, Smoky, Flame, Sooty, Flare, Ember, Ash, Tinder, Char, Scorch, and yours truly. When my eyes first opened, it was just in time to see spots popping out on the coats of my brothers and sisters. What was this?

I see spots, I said to my mum, whose name was Blaze.

Don't be alarmed, daughter my own. Dalmatians are born white. Our spots show up at two or three weeks.

I looked down at my legs and saw that they were covered with spots! Well, I'll be!

That's the way it is with Dals, Mum said.

We pups had a fine time, romping and playing

2

in our cozy nest of old flannel shirts. In that big, squirming pile of black-and-white fluff, I managed to stand out. When Plug and Sooty ganged up on little Ember, I snarled at them and drove them back behind the wash buckets. When little Flare got crowded off the last nipple, I gave Scorch a shove to make room. It was Michael Ryan, one of the firemen, who noticed. There came a day when he announced, "Hey, lads! We've got ourselves a proper keeper here, we have."

I didn't know what he meant. But I soon would.

When we pups were about eight weeks old, a man came and took Plug away. At first, I was over the moon. That little Plug was a heap of trouble. But the next day, another man came and took Sooty and Flare. And there wasn't a blessed thing I could do about it.

Within two weeks, every last one of my dear

brothers and sisters had been carted off.

Where have they all gone?

My mum told me, *There is a great demand for dogs among the fire stations of Chicago. Your brothers and sisters are helping meet that demand.*

Why can't they take Khan instead?

Khan was the chow chow dog at the butcher shop across the road. He was supposed to guard the store, but he preferred to chase horses. And he had a special fondness for fire horses. They drove him wild.

It's dogs like Khan who make dogs like us so necessary. You see, we are the horses' protectors.

Protectors? I said. *But we're so small compared to horses. How can that be?*

You'd be surprised, Mum said. *Horses might be big, but they are fearful by nature. And their brains are nowhere large enough to rule those huge bodies.*

Our job is to make them feel safe and secure. Why, there are those who say that a good Dalmatian is as necessary to the running of a station as a well-stoked steam engine.

Will they give me away, too? I asked.

No, Sparky. You're a keeper. We need you here. I'm not getting any younger, you know.

Well, then let's get started. If I had no one to play with, I might as well be useful.

But Mum said, *You're too young yet, dearie. There are things you need to learn. For a start, you must never do your business in the fire station.*

So I learned to hold it in until Michael let me out. Then I found my way into the dark spaces beneath the high wooden sidewalks. There, like a good dog, I answered nature's call as the people *tramp-tramp*ed above me.

Another of her lessons was *Pay attention around*

horses. *They don't know their own strength.*

That much I had already figured out for my-self. Horses had more power than they knew what to do with. Hadn't I once seen a horse knock an ax off a ledge with a sweep of her tail? I'd seen another who, with a mere shift of his weight, had squashed a kitten flat beneath his hoof. I had no intention of being knocked cockeyed or flattened to a pancake.

Mum said, *When a horse licks his lips, he's your friend. When he pins his ears back, head for the hills!*

She also said, *Always approach a horse from the side, with no quick movements. A horse can't see you when you are standing in front of him. His eyes are on the sides of his head. And horses do not like surprises.*

How well I knew this! One time, a fireman dragged a wooden chest out into the open to dig around for an ax handle. He forgot to put the chest back against the wall. When a mare came out of her stall for a brushing, she froze and would not move past it. From the look she gave that chest, you'd have thought it had sprouted horns and fangs. I asked Mum how in the world such timid and frightened beings could ever face something as fierce as fire.

It's all in the training, Mum said.

There were five horses in my fire station: one male as black as my spots, and four females as milky white as my coat. The male was, according to Mum, of a breed known as Percheron: big and strapping and sure-footed. The white mares were called Thoroughbreds and just as full of themselves as they could be. Every day, the horses were led out of their stalls and brushed down and fussed over and fed apples and treats.

Such was not the case for us. With dogs, it was all rough-and-tumble. The boys wrestled with us on the station floor. We played tug-of-war with ropes and fetch with sticks. They took us for long runs through the city. Sure, it was a fine way to learn the lay of the land. But I had to run hard and fast every day or else I'd get up to no good. Once, when it was raining too heavily to go out, I got hold of Michael's leather helmet and chewed it to a pulp. After that, you can be sure I never missed my run again, rain or shine.

Running wasn't just to keep me out of trouble. It was also for training. The first rule Michael drummed into me was *Never run ahead.*

"Your place is to the side of and slightly behind the horse," he explained. "You guide the animal and set the pace. You're also the horse's guardian. You dart out ahead and clear a path, chasing away those who would meddle. You're particularly needed when a horse is wearing blinkers."

Already, I knew that word. Blinkers are the part of a horse's bridle that covers the eyes and blocks his vision. The theory is that what the horse cannot see won't scare him. But blinkers also all but blind a horse. Fire dogs then act like an extra pair of eyes.

True to my training, I stayed to the side of and slightly behind Michael. I did it even though everything in me wanted to bound along before him.

I also followed Michael upstairs when it was time to eat. Off duty, the boys stayed with their own families elsewhere in the city. But while on duty, their home was the station. They slept upstairs in cots and ate their meals at the long wooden table nearby. Michael sat at one end, where I would hunker down next to him.

I watched the food go from his plate to his mouth. I licked my chops as I watched him chew and swallow. Oh, how my mouth watered! Sure,

I had been fed, but a bowlful of scraps was not enough for a growing girl!

Finally, one day, when I could stand it no longer, I barked—once, very sharply—and fixed Michael with a hard, glittering eye.

All up and down the table, the lads burst out laughing.

Michael said, "Okay, Chief, I can follow orders, too." And he tossed me a bit from his plate.

You might say that I wasn't the only one being trained at that fire station.

Once, when I was about four months old, one of the mares was out of her stall getting her daily brushing. Now was the time, I figured, to make my first move.

Just as Mum had taught me, I came up on the mare slowly and from the side. She was a sight to inspire awe, what with those four long stalk-like legs and the graceful and creamy upsweep of her belly soaring high above me. Her mouth was buried in a pile of hay. I heard crunching, grinding noises. The muscles beneath her skin twitched as I drew near.

I come in peace, I said softly.

I held my breath. Would I be toppled with a sweep of her mighty tail or squashed flat with a mighty hoof?

2

FIRE DANCE

The horse jerked her head up from the hay and glared at me. *Hasn't your mother told you not to bother a horse while she's at her hay?*

Sorry!

To show that I meant no harm, I touched the cold black tip of my nose, ever so gently, to the warm pink softness of hers.

Suddenly, two great puffs of wind shot out her nostrils, nearly blasting me off my feet.

W-what was that?! I sputtered and sneezed.

She threw back her head and whinnied. *A habit we horses have. Cleans out the system. Flushes out the hay dust and the mites. You should try it sometime.*

I often heard them huffing like this in their stalls, one right after another, like the steam locomotives lined up over in the rail yards where I sometimes ran with Michael.

My name is Sparky.

They call me Dumpling. I'm the senior member of the team whose proud duty it is to pull the Little Giant. *That's the steam engine—the most important piece of equipment in the station. I'm happy to call you friend, little dog. We horses need all the friends we can get.*

She cast a wary look around. Then she brought her head down close to mine. In a deep whisper, she added, *The whole world's out to get us.*

She went back to munching her hay.

The whole world?

Dumpling snorted bitterly. *Take my word for it.*

That could not be true, I said to myself. But I didn't want to bicker with her, so I said, *Don't worry. I'll protect you.*

The next morning at breakfast, I waited until the chorus of banging buckets had died back. When Joe the Stoker opened the door to the Percheron's stall to toss in some flakes of hay, I slipped past him inside.

Who let you in? the big brute asked, shaking loose some hay.

My heart skipped. Here was an animal who stood seventeen of a man's hands high at the shoulder. *I thought I'd drop in and bid you good day,* I said gamely.

Then a voice nearby nickered, *Don't throw a*

shoe, Butch. That's the pup I was telling you about. The keeper. Any keeper of Michael's is a keeper in my book.

I peered into the darkness next door. Beyond the bars, the whites of Dumpling's eyes flashed.

That's easy for you to say, Butch groused. *She's not standing in your stall.*

True enough, said Dumpling. *Everybody's got it in for horses.*

Take that chow chow across the street, said Butch.

If only someone would! Dumpling said wistfully. *Far, far away from here.*

Whenever we turn out for a fire, he's standing there waiting for me. That nasty black tongue and those sharp teeth rile me up every time. A shiver traveled up Butch's neck. *The Little Lion, the lads call him. I don't know what it means, but it sounds vicious.*

The Little Lion loves to chase after Butch, said

Dumpling to me. *Don't ask me why. But he never misses a chance.*

Doesn't my mother protect you? I asked.

She's up ahead, with the mares, said Butch. *So the devil takes the hindmost.*

It would be one thing if the devil barked, said Dumpling, *like a normal dog.*

Now that you mention it . . . , I said. I had never actually heard Khan bark.

It's unnatural, is what it is, said Butch. *A dog who doesn't bark.*

Just then, Joe opened the stall door, carrying a scoop of oats for Butch. He chuckled when he saw me. "Well, look who's paying social calls now. Off you go, missy, before the alarm goes off and your spots get trampled to wee speckles."

Nice meeting you, big fella! I said to Butch. And off I skedaddled.

When I asked Mum about Khan, she turned and showed me the scar above her tail.

The first time Khan chased after Butch, I bit him. He bit me back. Now we have an understanding. We steer clear of each other.

But Khan frightens Butch. He said so himself, I said.

Khan can be frightening. But he does no real harm, and he always drops back before the end of the block. We pick our battles, dearie, as you will learn soon enough. And don't you go getting any smart ideas. Stay away from the Little Lion. He's a strange-looking creature with even stranger ways.

It was the first time I had ever heard fear in my mum's voice.

In the days that followed, I met the other three mares, on a day when all four had been taken out for a grooming. I asked them about Khan and they tossed their manes and scoffed and snorted.

Safety in numbers, Sparky, said Daisy.

We gals stick together, said Maisy.

Twelve hooves are better than four, said Maybelle.

Riffraff, Dumpling snorted, then flushed her nostrils and set off a round of the same in the other gals.

As the weeks passed, I often sat in front of the station and watched Khan standing guard outside the butcher shop. Although he gave me the evil eye, he never set paw across the street.

The winter I turned one, the alarms were again coming fast and furious. This is as good a time as any to tell you that I knew ahead of time when the fire bell was going to ring. Don't ask me how. I'd get a peculiar tingling in my bones. I'd bark and dance around and, just like that—*clang! clang! clang!*—the bell would go off.

One afternoon, I was downstairs watching the lads play the game they called cards. There was Michael, who drove the steam engine, and Joe, who was its stoker. Then there was Sully, who drove the hose cart, and Mack and Jack, who were what they called pipemen—which means they handled the hoses. The five of them sat in a circle, their cards laid out on a board propped on their knees, near the *Little Giant,* where it was always toasty and warm.

The *Giant* had four spoked wheels—two enormous ones in back and two smaller ones up front. Michael kept the trim of those wheels spanking clean and brightly painted. But the boiler was her heart and soul.

It looked like an enormous milk can with a smokestack on top, all aglitter with brass fittings and nickel plate. Attached to the boiler was the pump, its pressure gauge like a big egg. On the site of a fire, Joe would stoke the fire, or feed coal to the flames in the boiler. That's why they called him the stoker. The boiler gave off steam that set the pump to churning. When the lads hooked a short hose called a taper to the nearest fireplug, the water from the city mains flowed through the taper into her pump. Pressure from the pump filled the fire hose and sent the water shooting out its nozzle, with Jack and Mack there to hold it and make sure the water hit its mark.

As everyone knows, you can't douse a raging fire simply by tossing water on it. The only way to reach a fire and kill it dead is to shoot it with water from a hose under pressure. Joe kept a small fire going in the boiler at all times, ready to stoke at a moment's notice.

There were fire alarm boxes all around the city. Each station had a lookout tower and its own bell. When one of the boys up in the tower spied smoke or flames, he'd ring the house bell. Other times, we'd get a telegraph from the central lookout in the courthouse tower, and then we'd ring our own bell.

Sully was shuffling the cards when I got that familiar tingling feeling. I took to my feet and started to bark and prance.

Michael looked up from his cards. "Game's over, laddies! The Chief's doing her Fire Dance."

By the time the bell rang, the lads were already on their feet, having stowed the card board.

How it got my blood up to watch them spring into action! The boys napping in the cots upstairs came pounding down the stairs, one after another. Everyone made a mad dash for the lockers, where they jumped into their gear: knee-high boots and helmets.

Meanwhile, the stall doors slid open automatically, triggered by the bell, and the horses sprang out and looked lively. They trotted up before their rigs: the mares to the steamer, Butch to the hose cart. The next moment, the collars and harnesses hanging from the ceiling dropped down onto their necks and backs. Not a one of them ever flinched. That was training for you! Mack came along and closed the collars. Jack hitched them up and snapped on the reins and blinkers. The boys piled onto the vehicles, the drivers grabbed the reins, and off they raced.

As for me, I stood there and watched them tear off down the street, wishing with all my heart that I could go with them.

KHAN'S SAD TALE

I curled up beneath the stairs. Fat Belle, the ratter, slinked over and rubbed herself against the bottom step.

Look who's sulking, she said.

I'm not sulking.

You'd fool me, said the ratter.

I heaved a sigh. *They've all gone off to the fire, and I'm stuck here with you and the mice.*

I don't know why you're so eager to join them. Before you were born, the general store down the street caught fire. It burned so hot it singed my whiskers. But it was far worse for one of the lads. A burning timber fell and crushed the life clean out of him.

I shivered and burrowed my head deeper into my tail.

All I'm saying, said Belle, *is that fire is no friend of yours. It's downright dangerous!*

With that, she padded upstairs.

Sometime after I had dropped off to sleep, I awoke to a strange noise. I cracked open an eye.

Someone had entered the fire station!

He wore a long coat and a hat pulled low over his eyes. Slowly, he moved over to the wall of lockers. Opening the first door, he rooted around. I watched him work his way down the row, opening and shutting doors, stuffing the pockets of his coat.

I leaped to my feet. Every black and white hair on my back stood on end as I puffed myself up and faced the intruder with eyes ablaze.

He gaped, hands reaching for the ceiling. "Easy now, Spot," he said, backing away.

I growled, *My name isn't Spot.*

Behind him was a bale of hay. I was happy to watch him trip over it and topple backward, his head hitting the edge of a toolbox.

I ran over and sniffed at him. He was still breathing, but he was out cold. I sat down next to him and stood guard.

That was where the boys found me when they returned from the call. The four gals, blackened with soot and smelling of wet fur and charred wood, trotted into the station. They pulled up short and whinnied with surprise.

Michael jumped down from the rig. "So we have ourselves a visitor, do we?"

He stood over the man, who groaned low and began to stir.

Michael knelt down and went through the man's pockets, removing four billfolds, two pocket watches, a shiny medal on a chain, and a locket filled with pictures of Joe's children.

"See here, Chief," he said to me, "if you're old enough to nab a thief, you're sure enough ready to become a Smoke-Eater."

I knew about smoke. I sniffed it on the crew when they came home after answering a call. No matter how hard they washed and scrubbed afterward, they never seemed to get rid of it. It clung to their hair and fur and skin and clothes. It was in the air we breathed. But of fire, I knew little.

One day, Michael flung open the *Giant*'s boiler door. I shrank back from the heat and the brightness.

"That, my little spotted Dal pal, is fire."

I gazed into the boiler's glowing maw. Tongues of flame wagged at me.

Hey, little miss, the coals hissed.

The flames snapped and spat, *Come closer.*

I poked my head forward and a flaming tongue

flicked out and licked the tip of my nose. I pulled back with a yelp of pain.

Gotcha! the fire cackled.

Crouching, I barked at the fire. *You'll never catch me again!* I carried on until my throat was raw and the flames had died down. Michael shut the boiler door and brushed off his hands.

With a huff, I threw myself down on the floor and dropped my nose onto my paws.

"There, there, now." Michael sat beside me and stroked my back. "Fire can be a helpful friend, Chief. It warms homes and cooks food and stokes the boilers that run steam engines, like the *Little Giant* here. But fire can also destroy property and lives. Fire can be good and fire can be bad, but fire is never to be trusted and always to be feared and respected. If you've learned that lesson, I think you might be ready for a dry run."

On days when there were no fires, Michael hitched the mares up to the *Giant* and took them out for a spin. A dry run, he called it. But even though I knew there would be no fire, the threat of the Little Lion was real.

Mum gave me some pointers. *When Khan comes charging out at you, don't flinch. Don't stop, don't bark, don't challenge him, and, above all, don't ever look him in the eye. Pretend he isn't there. By the time you get to the corner, he will have fallen back.*

But nothing could have prepared me for the fury with which the Little Lion came at me.

His fur bristled and his eyes were as shiny as coals, his black tongue lolling like a razor strop. He made a harsh rasping sound in his throat that froze the blood in my veins. I felt his breath, hot and ragged, on my tail. I stayed on Daisy's outside flank. Desperate to escape, I whipped the mares into a gallop. With a screech of wheels, the *Little Giant* careened around the corner onto Clinton.

As the engine tipped up onto her outside wheels, Michael shouted, "Easy, now, Chief!" He pulled hard on the reins. The horses slowed. The *Giant* righted herself.

I risked a look over my shoulder. Khan stood, panting, on the corner of Clinton and Maxwell.

Mercy me! said Daisy.

Don't ever do that to us again! said Maisy.

That was worse than being chased by the chow chow! said Maybelle.

And a lot more dangerous, said Dumpling.

Sorry, ladies, I said. *I lost my head. It won't happen again.*

And it did not, which was a very good thing because, all too soon, I would be making a real run.

It started with that familiar tingling in my bones. I went into my Fire Dance. And the bell went off.

But this was no ordinary bell.

This is it, Sparky, said my mum. *Your first fire.*

The boys came pounding down the stairs, still chewing their breakfast. The stall doors sprang open and the horses sprang forth. Mack buckled the collars and snapped on the blinkers. Jack clipped on the harness and reins. Joe threw open the wide wooden doors. The lads clambered onto the equipment, Michael took up the reins, and the mares pulled out, escorted by my mum.

I took my position next to Butch as we brought up the rear with the hose cart. It had rained during the night, and the streets were slick.

True to form, Khan came flying after me. When we neared the first intersection, the chow chow skidded—and collided with the rear wheel!

"Look out, mutt!" Sully shouted.

Khan's leg got snagged in the spokes. The wheel

whipped him around, then flung him off into the gutter. The hose cart rolled on. I slid to a halt.

Khan lay there, dazed and bleeding.

While the rigs rolled on, I ran back a ways to check on him.

Are you all right? I asked.

I got no answer.

See here, I said, *I'll get someone if you need help.*

Finally, in a low rasp, he said, *I reckon I'll live.*

Good, I said.

I was just about to take my leave when I heard him say, *All I ever wanted was to go to a fire.*

Then that's what you should do, I said. *But stop bothering us.*

It's never been my intention to cause bother. It's just that I have trouble controlling my excitement at the sound of the bell. The first time I ran off to a fire, the butcher beat me. So I learned my lesson. I figured if I couldn't go to a fire, at least I could send the rest of you off with a few lively barks. But my master got sick of me barking. One day, he walloped me in the neck with a meat saw. Killed my bark dead. Now I can hardly speak. But no one can keep me from running.

What a tale of woe! But there was nothing I could do for him. My place was with the crew. I left Khan where he lay and ran to catch up with Butch.

People had started to cross the street in front of him. I darted out, barking, and drove them back onto the sidewalk.

On the next block, two dogs charged out to challenge the mares. *Private property,* they snarled.

Ease off, fellows, Mum told them. *We're only passing through.*

Everyone else gave us a wide berth. Children jumped up and down. Ladies stopped and waved their handkerchiefs. Men cheered and saluted. I felt a surge of pride.

A few blocks down the road, my nose began to twitch. The stench soon stung my nostrils. We rounded the corner and there it was.

My first fire!

SMOKE-EATER

A rooming house had gone up in flames. Michael drove the team of four mares so close to the blaze, I thought he was going to run the gals right onto the front porch! He jumped out, unhitched the team, and led them across the street and partway down the block. Sully unfastened Butch from the hose cart and parked us across the street from the fire.

Mum left the gals long enough to come and check on me.

I've never been better, I told her. I was so excited to be there!

She was panting and gulping to catch her breath.

What about you, Mum? I asked. *Are you all right?*

I'm fine, she said. *It's just that . . . a dog who's eaten . . . as much smoke and soot as me . . . gets a little winded . . . now and then.*

I looked at the four mares down the block. They were waiting anxiously for Mum's return. *Why do we have to split up like this?* I said. *Why can't we all stand together?*

Mum explained to me, panting all the while, that Butch was the lead horse. If he panicked and ran, the others would follow. Broken up into two groups, they acted less like a herd and more like a bunch of professionals who would remember their training: to stay put and remain calm. *And if they forget . . . our job is to step up and remind them.*

With that, she returned to her post.

The flames crackled and leaped. Like the rest of the city, the rooming house was made of wood and built to burn. Most of the buildings in Chicago were made of wood. And there's nothing that fire loves better than wood. Chicago had been built over a swamp and clay that drained poorly. To stay above the muck, the city had put in high wooden sidewalks. As if all that weren't enough, some of the streets were paved with blocks of oily pine.

In his gloomiest moments, Michael said that it was just a matter of time before a fire destroyed the entire city. The Big Burn, he called it.

I tried to wipe these thoughts from my mind as I watched Sully unwinding the hose from the reel, hitching one end up to the steamer. Michael found a fireplug, then attached the taper hose. Joe

stoked the boiler fire. Dark smoke came billowing
out of her stack. Soon, her pump began to churn.
The hose from the fireplug began to swell with water pumped from the mains. Water came spurting

out the nozzle. The pressure was so powerful that Mack and Jack had to wrestle with the hose. Finally getting it under control, they shot a steady stream of water into the blazing heart of the fire.

I felt the harsh heat of it on my face.

Do you ever get used to it? I asked Butch.

Never, he said with a nervous stomp. *Say, is my mane on fire? I thought I felt an ember land on my neck.*

I examined his mane from ears to shoulders. *You look fine,* I said.

He cast a glance behind us. *I wish all these nosy people would go away.*

A crowd had gathered on the sidewalk behind us. Some, clutching whatever possessions had come to hand when they first smelled the smoke, had escaped from the rooming house. Others had no business here. They stared, wide-eyed, into the flames, laughing and pointing. They had even brought refreshments. For these people, fire was *entertainment.*

Fire Fiends, the lads called them.

Michael came and shooed them away. But the Fiends just crept back.

Then suddenly, my ears perked. Above the din, I heard a faint voice calling, "Help! Help me!"

An old woman leaned out of a top-floor window, clutching a cat.

I ran to Michael and barked.

"I know, Chief. Fire's a scary business," he said.

I barked louder. *You don't understand!*

He waved me away.

But I would not be put off. I caught the cuff of his jacket in my teeth and dragged him across the street. Then I barked at the window. Michael looked up and gasped.

"Get out your ladder, boys!" he shouted to
the crew who had just arrived. "There's a woman
trapped on the top floor."

Pulled by two giant draft horses, the wagon

called the hook-and-ladder extended halfway down the block—longer and heavier than either of our rigs.

"Mack and Jack!" Michael shouted. "Tamp down those flames! Clear the way for the ladder."

My lads redirected the hose's spray to a spot just beneath the window while the newly arrived crew set their ladder up against the house.

One man held the bottom while another scrambled up. He reached in and dragged the woman over the sill. The cat clawed and fought, but the woman held fast to it. One hand on the lady's back and the other on the ladder, the man climbed down. Neighbors wrapped the woman in blankets and led her off to safety.

Hours later, the rooming house was nothing but a charred ruin. The other crew stacked its ladders back on the wagon, hitched up the horses, and hauled off down the street. Sully wound the hose onto the reel. Michael unfastened the taper from the fireplug. The lads moved slowly, like old men. Back to the fire station we dragged.

There, the lads peeled off their gear. They honked their noses and emptied black goo into their handkerchiefs. As for me, my eyes burned and my chest felt heavy.

Well, Sparky, you did it, said Mum, black drool dripping from her jaw.

With what was left of my strength, I wagged my tail. It was official now: I was a Smoke-Eater.

But if that fire was my first, it would prove to be Khan's last. The following day, he was absent from his post in front of the butcher shop. When the bell next rang, there was no Little Lion dogging the horses' heels.

At first, the horses didn't believe he was gone

for good. A horse, once frightened, rarely forgets. Khan was the subject of endless discussions.

He probably just ran away, Daisy said one day when the horses were standing in the crossties, being hosed down.

Who cares? said Maisy and Dumpling, shaking the water off their coats.

Good riddance to bad rubbish, I say, said Maybelle, knocking the soapsuds off her mane with a flip of her head.

I don't think he was all that bad, I said.

All four mares whipped their heads around at once to stare at me.

Of course he was bad, said Daisy.

He was a bad egg, said Maisy.

A right tosser, said Maybelle and Dumpling.

He wasn't really, I insisted. *I think he was just sad that he couldn't be a fire dog.*

It was then I told them what Khan had said, how all he had ever wanted was to go to a fire. *And the one time he did go, his master beat him. And when he got sick of his barking, he walloped Khan in the neck with a meat saw and killed his bark. How would you feel if you lost your whinny?*

Wide-eyed, the horses shook their heads until the buckles of their lead halters rattled.

The seasons passed, I did my dance, and the fire bell kept ringing. With every call answered, I got better at my job. By the time I was three years old, I had helped fight more than a hundred fires. Each fire was different, challenging the lads in a new way. But the fire that broke out one late summer's day was especially bad and had, for the Maxwell Street station, serious consequences.

It started in a lumber warehouse on the river.

The flames quickly ate their way up the pillars into the ceiling beams. Soon, the roof came crashing down. Fortunately, none of the boys were inside. They had given up by then and were just standing around, waiting for the fire to burn itself out. That's the way it went sometimes.

On our way back to the station, I noticed Dumpling limping. I caught up with her.

I twisted my dad-blamed leg, she muttered.

When the roof caved in, she explained, she had spooked and shied to the side.

I guess even a seasoned fire horse could lose her head now and then.

I walked with her the last few blocks.

When we got there, Michael ran his hands over Dumpling's leg. I touched it with my nose. It was hot!

The next day, the doc came and bathed her leg in medicine and wrapped it in clean rags. He told Michael to soak it.

I'm done for, Dumpling said, standing with her lame leg in a bucket. *I'm as useless as a buggy in a bog. It's a bullet in the head for me.*

Don't say that! I scolded. But I was scared for her, too.

When the doc came back to look at Dumpling, he shook his head. "This horse has gone to her last fire."

Flustered, the other mares paced in their stalls.

What will become of Dumpling? said Daisy.

Who will help us pull the Giant? said Maisy.

Stop your fussing, ladies, said Butch. *Some steamers have only two horses to pull them.*

Upstairs, the lads worried, too. There wasn't

51

enough money on hand to buy a new horse.

Where will Dumpling go? I asked my mum as we sat beneath the table and worried and panted.

She'll be moving on to her Greater Reward.

Greater Reward? I asked. *What's that?*

I have no idea, said Mum. *But that's where horses go when they're finished here. I must say I've never liked the sound of it.*

Nor did I.

CINDY

The next day, Michael drove up to the station in a buckboard. Nestled next to him was his twelve-year-old daughter, Lizzy. We all knew and loved Lizzy. And how could we not? She never visited without bringing home-baked goodies for the horses, bones for us Dals, and a jar of buttermilk for Fat Belle. Some people are dog lovers. Others love cats. Still others are soft on horses. But Lizzy loved *all* animals.

Lizzy had a special air about her. A deep stillness. And out of that stillness there came an understanding of us animals. It was as if she gazed into our hearts and minds and saw the things that hurt us or frightened us or haunted our dreams. She had an especially knowing way with horses. Sometimes, when one of the horses was off, Michael would bring in Lizzy instead of the doc. That's how much everyone trusted this girl and her special gift.

Today, we were all in a state and Lizzy, in her usual way, knew exactly why.

"You're afraid my father is going to have Dumpling destroyed," she said as she stroked Dumpling's mane.

I looked up and panted. How did she know?

She smiled at me. "I can tell by the way you're all carrying on."

It was true. The mares were pacing, Butch was hiding in the back of his stall (as if a Percheron could ever hide!), and Mum and I were too nervous to start in on our bones.

"Well, you can all stop worrying," she told us. "We're taking Dumpling to live at my uncle Finn's Second Chance Farm. He offers a paddock of sweet grass to horses that retire from fighting fires. It's their Greater Reward for risking their lives for the city of Chicago."

The horses all blew out with relief. Mum and I settled down with our bones.

Shortly after this, Michael secured Dumpling to the rear of the buckboard and off they went, Dumpling limping merrily along behind. The rest of us went back to our business, trying not to look at the empty stall.

Imagine our surprise when, at the end of the day, Michael showed up with a dapple-gray Percheron hitched to the back of the buckboard.

Most horses have a look in their eye that says, *The whole world's out to get me.* But this one's said, *I'm out to get the whole world!*

What was Michael Ryan *thinking*?

"Welcome to your new home, Cinders," said Michael, untying the horse from the buckboard.

Michael started to take her to Dumpling's old stall, but the newcomer wanted no part of it. She planted her big hooves and refused to move.

"*Now* what?" said Joe, throwing up his hands.

"Lizzy could get her to go in there," Michael muttered. "But she's got school tomorrow, so I dropped her off at home. She swore Cinders would make a fine fire horse, and when it comes to horses, Lizzy is never wrong."

"I thought we agreed we had enough horses for now," Joe said.

"If, God forbid, something happens to Butch, we've got backup," said Michael.

The harder Michael tugged on the lead rope, the deeper the Percheron dug in her heels.

I watched from the shadows. What would happen if the alarm went off? We couldn't have this stubborn mule blocking the way.

"Now, Joe," Michael said, "get behind her and push."

"Is this horse even *broke*?" Joe asked as he leaned into the mare's hind end.

Michael said, "Broke *and* trained. She just needs to adjust. I see now I should have had Lizzy stay. She'd get this horse moving, meek as a lamb."

"Yeah, but Lizzy can't live here, and now this meek lamb is *our* problem."

"Keep pushing, Joe!" Michael said.

"Sakes alive, Michael Ryan! She's a ton of horseflesh. If she doesn't want to move, no amount of pushing will get her going. How much did we pay for her, may I ask?"

"She was free," said Michael.

"Well, there you go. You get what you pay for," said Joe.

"She's a valuable animal, she is. Trained Percherons cost a fortune. Fetch a bucket of feed now and go stand in her stall, like a good lad," said Michael.

Joe stood in the mouth of the stall and banged the bucket with the scoop. "Come and get it!" he shouted.

The other horses began to stomp and mutter.

That horse is plum crazy! said Daisy.

And nasty! said Maisy.

She's got an ornery look in her eye, said Maybelle.

I did not disagree. I started barking. Mum joined in.

"Hush, gals," Michael said. "You're not being much of a help, are you now?"

He was right. All the noise only drove the mare farther away from the stall, dragging Michael along with her. It wasn't long before the horse had pulled Michael out into the middle of the street.

A wagon driver with a team of eight pulling a load of coal ground to a stop. "Get that stupid horse out of our way!" he shouted.

"I'm doing the best I can, sir!" said Michael.

From the other direction, a tinker's wagon came to a halt. "See here! What's the holdup? I have business down the road!" the tinker shouted.

On the sidewalk, crowds gathered to watch.

One of them said, "Hey! Isn't that the horse that killed Old Man Muller last winter?"

"A man-killer?" someone else shouted. "Somebody get me a shotgun. I'll take care of her."

More wagons piled up. Horses stomped and drivers tapped their whips angrily.

"Chief!" Michael called to me. "Get out here!"

I went to him.

"Make yourself useful, girl. Calm this horse down and drive her into her stall."

Before I did anything, that horse was going to get a piece of my mind.

Look, missy, I said, fixing her with my sternest look. *I don't know how you do things where you come from. But here we don't carry on this way. Any minute now, that bell is going to ring and we'll be rushing off to do serious work. This is no place to throw silly tantrums.*

The horse licked and chewed, a sign that she was at least willing to listen. So I got behind her and snapped my jaws. One rear leg lifted. The other three hooves started moving forward.

"Atta girl! Keep at it," Michael said.

Step by step, I drove Cinders back into the fire station.

Joe saw us coming. He hung up the bucket and skipped aside as I sent Cinders clomping into the stall.

Later, upstairs, as I lay beneath the wooden table, voices were raised in argument.

"What's the idea bringing a man-killer into our station?" Jack asked.

"Ain't it enough that we fight fires?" said Mack. "Now we got a rogue horse to fight, too?"

Michael's voice was calm. "Lizzy says the horse has a good heart. And Lizzy knows animals better than anyone I know. A little tender loving care, some training, and we've got ourselves a brand-new fire horse, free of charge, haven't we now?"

The boys grumbled and settled down. But I could tell they didn't like it any more than I did.

Man-Killer, they had called her in the street. *Man-Killer,* they had called her on the second floor. *Man-Killer,* the other horses muttered in their stalls. But it dawned on me: was it possible that Cinders, like Khan, wasn't bad so much as unhappy and misunderstood?

I paid her a visit one morning.

Say, is it true what they say? That you're a man-killer? I asked, bold as you please.

With a shuffle of hooves, she wheeled slowly around to face me.

I'm no man-killer! she said in a voice filled with a deep sadness that made my heart ache.

Is that a fact? Well, suppose you tell me your side

of the story, I said. *I'm all ears and a dozen spots.*

With a heavy sigh, Cinders began: *A surprise snowstorm blew in the night my master and I were returning from business in the city. I pulled the sled all night through the deep and icy snow. The old man was so still and quiet I feared he had frozen to death. We were nearly through the home gate when he stood up and clutched his heart. Then he groaned and pitched forward onto the ground near my feet. I didn't dare move a muscle for fear of trampling him. His wife and sons came running from the house. They tugged at me and shouted at me, and one of them hit me with a shovel.*

Then what happened? I asked.

I moved. And I stepped on the old man, she replied glumly. *Next thing I knew, someone drove me into a barn stall. I'd never in my life been in a barn, much less a stall. I had spent my whole life out in the fresh air. That's why I made such a fuss when I first came here. I never wanted to go back into a stall.*

Stalls are a fact of life for city horses, I said.

That may be true, but I was in a stall when the old man's son came in with a gun and fixed to shoot me. He wanted me to pay for killing his father.

I shivered. That must have been terrifying!

Luckily, he couldn't bring himself to do it. But it scared the life out of me. After that, things got even worse. By the time Finn found me, I was living in a junkyard, half-starved. He had come to rescue me, but I didn't know it then. I thought he meant to hurt me. I tried to scare him off. You don't know what it's like to be treated like a killer. It drives you a little crazy after a while. You get so you're even afraid of yourself.

I sat down and scratched a flea and thought.

I'll tell you what I think, I began.

Yes? she said, the light in her eyes building like the fire in the *Giant*'s boiler.

I think this fire station is as good a place as any for you to get a fresh start. If you give us a chance, we'll give you one.

THE RED FLASH

The very next day, Michael got a lead rope and halter and opened Cinders's stall door. "All right, then, Cinders," he said. "Are you ready to learn how to be a fire horse and do my Lizzy proud?"

Cinders bowed her head and let Michael slip on the halter.

Cinders caught on quickly to the training. After all, she had spent weeks watching what the other horses did when the bell went off. When it became clear that she was a smart, teachable horse, the other lads came around. Before long, they were sneaking her apples and calling her Cindy. And the great thing about this horse was that she didn't use blinkers. She wouldn't have anything to do with them. Now *that's* what I call a sensible animal.

One day, when Cinders was out of the stall being groomed, she asked me, *So, now that I've told you my big secret, can you tell me yours?*

What secret? I asked.

I've noticed that every time you dance around and bark, the bell rings, she said. *How do you do it?*

I grinned. She actually thought I caused the bell to ring. That was a horse for you. They have the strangest sense of cause and effect.

I don't make it ring. I just know when it's going

to go off. I get a tingling feeling in my bones.

Do you think that maybe someday I'll get that feeling, too?

You never know, I said, but I seriously doubted it. After all, I was a fire dog and she was just a horse.

Cinders's training continued through the fall to winter to spring and on into the following summer. You'd think that, after nearly a year of drilling, she'd be as ready as Freddie. But the way the lads saw it, a horse had to do a thing hundreds of times for the training to really sink in. So when the fire bell rang, day after day, Cinders stayed in her stall.

The summer of '71 had been crackling hot and dry. Only five inches of rain had fallen. Autumn brought little relief. September had been unseasonably warm with less than an inch of rain. So far, October boded no better. Chicago was as dry and parched as the nose of a feverish pooch. To add to everyone's unease, a wind from the southwest had picked up, bringing with it the stench of the stockyards.

When the bell went off on Saturday following a week that was chockablock with alarms, the boys were exhausted. The fire started in a small wood-working factory on the West Side. On the same street were a paper box factory, a slew of saloons, and several lumberyards where mountains of coal were stored for the winter. Was it any wonder the insurance men had already dubbed this neck of the woods the "Red Flash"?

We were the first company to arrive. The fire had already eaten its way through the mill and was leaping north, thanks to the wind.

Michael unhitched the mares and led them away. Then he fastened the taper to the fireplug. After stoking the fire, Joe started the pump. Mack and Jack grabbed the nozzle and began pouring hundreds of gallons of water per minute onto the fire.

After an hour of spraying, the fire was stronger than ever—and spreading. The assistant fire marshal on the West Side went to Michael and said, "Your boys need help!"

"That they do, Matt!" Michael said.

The fire marshal pulled the second alarm. Soon, engines from nearby districts arrived. Boys ran around searching for plugs. The *Chicago* galloped over from the South Side. The engineer staked out a spot on the north front of the fire. He hooked up a taper and got their pump going. Immediately, his hose burst at the seams. While he and his lads replaced the broken link, the fire leaped across the street and continued on its blazing way northward.

Flames soon devoured the box factory. The roof

caved in with a loud *whoosh*. Embers rained down. Beneath the smell of burning paper and wood, I caught a whiff of singed horsehair.

A cluster of sparks had landed on Butch's back. He started to pitch and buck.

Get down and roll! I told the poor devil.

He folded his legs and went down onto his back, rolling. Climbing to his feet, he shook off the last sparks. *Close call!*

The air was thick with burning embers. The other horses stomped and shifted, fearful of suffering Butch's fate. Thoughtful strangers came and moved the horses farther down the block. But no sooner were they relocated than they had to be moved again. The fire was chasing after us.

The assistant marshal ran to sound the third alarm. The whole city knew what that meant: "fire out of control." It brought all available firemen and equipment racing to the scene, including the muckety-mucks from the fire commission: the first and second assistant fire marshals from the South and the North, as well as the biggest brass of them all—the one they called Chief Williams.

A giant of a man, Williams stalked up to the fire and glared at it as if daring it to blink first. He was clad in high boots, a long black coat, and a pointed cap. He had an impressive set of bushy whiskers, and it was small wonder they never caught fire. Clenched in his fist was a brass speaking trumpet. He swung around and spoke through it, his voice booming above the fire's roar.

"Form a big circle, lads! Surround the fire! Contain it and don't let it spread!"

The crews moved their equipment to form a giant ring around the fire. Soon, hoses were spraying it from all sides.

Williams ordered nearby structures to be soaked to keep the fire from spreading. The hook-and-ladder boys took up axes and chopped down fences, shacks, sidewalks, outhouses—anything that might fuel the fire. In the nearby train yards, gangs of volunteers put their shoulders to the railroad cars and shoved them down the tracks, away from the flames.

I watched as the boys dragged the *Chicago* ever closer to the fire. It was the only way they could reach the flames, given how little hose they had left. Suddenly, the roof of the lumber warehouse collapsed in an explosion of sparks. The boys scrambled to pull the *Chicago* clear.

As the fire lit up the night sky, Fire Fiends came swarming in. They crowded the rooftops across the river. They shimmied up the masts of the ships on the river. They crammed the nearby sidewalks.

The roof of one building collapsed beneath the weight of them. Police and volunteers blocked off the Adams Street Bridge to prevent more Fiends from crossing the river just as the bridge burst into flame. The steamer *Titsworth* came charging over the burning bridge, steamer and crew running right through the fire, whiskers and manes aflame.

In the early hours of the morning, the lads finally got the fire under control. Four blocks of warehouses and buildings had been destroyed. The fire was still smoldering when the men, horses, and dogs of the Maxwell Street station packed up and went home. I noticed that Mum was limping badly.

Oh, daughter, I burned my paw pads, she said.

She could barely make it up the stairs when we went to get some grub.

After we ate, I left her resting by the stove and came back downstairs. The horses were tucked in

their stalls except for Butch and Cinders. Butch was in the crossties and Sully was tending him. Cinders was standing with her nose pressed into Sully's shoulder. I smelled the sharp scent of burnt horseflesh. It seemed that poor Butch had gotten badly hurt, after all.

Cinders was ready to take action if Sully did anything to cause Butch more pain. Now one of the herd, she was protecting a fellow in a weak moment. Bless her gallant heart!

Michael joined us and examined the wounds. The two men shook their heads.

"I don't know, Mike. These burns are bad. I think we need to put Butch on the Sick List."

"Sure, it's the right thing to do," said Michael, "even though that leaves us down one horse."

"I guess we'll just have to manage with what we've got," said Sully.

"All I can say," said Michael, "is there had better not be any more fires in this town until he's all healed up."

Little did we know that we were hours away from the biggest, hottest burn the city would ever see.

THE BIG BURN

Later that same day, Joe and I were on watch in the lookout tower. Michael had gone off to join some friends for dinner. Most of the other boys were still asleep in their cots, all done in from battling the Red Flash. As Joe gazed northward, he pointed. "Sparks, old gal, is that smoke?"

I barked. *You bet it is!*

He called down to Jack, the only other man awake. Jack came up to join us.

"Tell me, are those the smoldering remains of the Red Flash—or something new?" Joe asked his brother fireman.

Jack craned his neck. "Lord help us all. It's a new one!"

Jack rang the bell. For once, perhaps because I was bone-weary, I didn't even dance.

The boys groaned and sat up in their cots. Some of them hadn't even cleaned up yet from the earlier fire. Over by the stove, Mum lifted her head. *Another fire? So soon?* she whimpered.

Go back to sleep, I told her. *I'll cover for you.*

Thank you, dearie. She dropped her head back down on her paws.

Stupid with sleep, the men staggered down the stairs. Then came the heavy clip-clopping of the horses. The boys fumbled into their gear. A sorrier-looking bunch you never laid eyes on.

All except Cinders. The boys must have decided that, ready or not, she was going, because her door had been rigged to open. Like a spring colt, she danced into place before the hose cart.

"I'm glad *somebody* around here's got some spunk," Sully said as he snapped on Cinders's reins and hitched her to the hose wagon.

From his stall, Butch raised his head and muttered, *A word to the wise, Sparky. Stay close to the greenhorn tonight.*

Didn't I know it! Her first fire and she hadn't even finished training. I would stick to her like a cocklebur.

As we pulled out, the big bell in the courthouse tower tolled. Sully shook his head in disgust. The bell "spoke" to the city's firemen in code and told them where the fire was. He said, "What's the matter with those people in the tower? The fire's farther north than that."

Had we followed the alarm code, we would have headed south. Knowing better, we went north toward DeKoven and Jefferson, where we had seen the flames.

The lads had to hold on to their hats to keep them from blowing off. "This wind will make for a fierce burn!" Jack said.

Sully nodded gloomily.

Up ahead, a man called out to Sully, "I see you've got yourself a fine new dappled horse!"

Sully called back, "That I do! This is her first fire."

"Good luck to the both of you!" the man said.

As we neared the scene, a man came running up the street with a baby in his arms. A cow and a calf soon came loping after them.

Then I saw it. A big barn was swallowed up by flames, as were at least six other barns and houses.

It looked like we were the first to arrive.

My boys took a plug at the southwest corner. They dragged the hose between two houses and set themselves up in an alley behind the fire. Better late than never, Michael came running down the street, still buttoning up his jacket.

"Where is the *Williams*?" he shouted. "Where is the *J. B. Rice*?"

The *Williams* and the *Rice* were two of the newest, biggest steam engines in the city, able to pour seven hundred and nine hundred pounds of water a minute, respectively. They were from fire stations nearby. Michael was right: they should have been there.

"Some fool in the courthouse sounded the wrong alarm," said Joe. "The only reason we're here is we *saw* the fire from the lookout."

The courthouse—which had a view of the entire city—boasted a system of alarms that went to all the stations in Chicago. When the lookout there spied a fire, he sounded an alarm to alert the nearest fire station and telegraphed them, too. The system also worked the other way around. When fires broke out, people in the city could alert the courthouse from the nearest station or firebox. But for some reason, on this night, both the courthouse lookout and local folk were confused. Time and again, the wrong alarms went off. Firemen were wandering all over the city searching for the blaze. It was another thirty minutes or so before the other fire companies began to arrive, but by then the fire had gotten a deadly head start.

I kept a steady eye on Cinders. Wind whipping her mane, she shifted nervously.

Is there always this much confusion? she fretted.

No, tonight's different, I said. *Everything's going wrong. The lads are tired, the equipment is dirty, and the alarms are all wrong. The wind is the worst I've ever seen. You watch yourself, Cinders. If the wind blows an ember on you, shake it off or drop and roll. You don't want to wind up like poor Butch.*

Cinders snorted and shook herself down from mane to hooves, as if she were throwing off a shower of embers.

That's the idea, big girl, I told her. *Listen, I'm spread thin tonight, what with Mum being on the Sick List. I need to check on the Thoroughbreds. Will you be all right by yourself, Cinders?*

Please don't go! she said.

I found the mares almost as nervous as Cinders.

This is a bad burn, said Daisy.

It's spreading fast, said Maisy.

Chief Williams just got here, said Maybelle. *That means it's really bad.*

More and more men and equipment—steam

engines, hose carts, and hook-and-ladder rigs—
kept pulling in. The steamer *Chicago* hooked up to
a plug at Forquer and Jefferson. The steamer *Economy* set itself up north of the fire. And the steamer
Illinois found a plug at the corner of Des Plaines
and Taylor.

Men ran to and fro, shouting. The mares and I
watched and worried. From the sound of his voice,
Chief Williams was worried, too.

"Hold fast to her, Charley!" he hollered to the
man holding a hose.

Charley shouted, "Chief, I don't believe I can
stand it."

"Stand it as long as you can, lad!" Williams said.

Another man went up to Charley and said,
"This fire is mighty hot."

"That it is, my friend!" Charley agreed.

The friend went and brought back a door.

Holding the hosepipe in one hand, Charley used the door as a heat shield while he sprayed the fire.

But the door soon burst into flame. Charley kicked it aside. His boots and clothes were smoking. His leather hat had melted onto his head. His face was as red as cured ham.

The chief got a look at him and said, "Come away from the fire, Charley. Wet the other side of the street and keep it from burning."

Charley turned the hose around, soaking me and the mares. But we didn't mind. The embers that landed on us now fizzled out instead of catching fire.

Daisy raised her voice above the noise. *This is getting bad!*

Maisy said, *The fire is coming closer to us!*

What if the men are too busy to take care of us? Maybelle said.

If we have to, we'll cut and run, Daisy said in a shriek so loud that Cinders heard her from half a block away.

Cinders cried out, *Don't leave without me!*

Nobody's going anywhere! I said to the herd. *Everybody, stay calm! I'm going to take a look around and see what's going on. Try to keep your heads while I'm gone.*

Come back soon! The mares' call followed me as I ran down the road.

In all the excitement, I am ashamed to say I forgot my promise to stick to the greenhorn like a cocklebur.

DOGNAPPED!

The fire spread rapidly northward. Assistant marshals from the north, south, and west had arrived. The boys with the steamer *Titsworth* and the hose cart *Tempest* had set themselves up to the west to keep the flames from crossing Jefferson. The *Waubansia*, the *Long John*, the *Sherman*, and the *Economy* steamers worked to head off the fire on the north side. The hook-and-ladder boys swung their axes and chopped down fences and sheds, destroying anything that might feed the flames.

The fire huffed like a hungry monster, growing bigger with every breath it drew. I had never seen anything like it. The flames exploded and skipped from building to building and block to block. They leaped from one side of the street to the other. Whirlwinds of fire broke off and whipped down the street, igniting everything in their path.

Streets that had been quiet and empty moments ago were now crammed with people carrying their worldly goods or pushing them in carts. People leaned out windows, screaming. I turned my head away as the wind gusted and sent a blizzard of hot red snowflakes into my face. It was blowing northeast, toward the business district: the very heart of the city.

The Fire Fiends had come out in droves. Policemen riding horses tried to hold them back, but there were too many of them. One group had gathered to watch on top of a teetering pile of lumber. They craned their heads. One of them pointed and shouted, "Look! An ember has just landed on the steeple of St. Paul's!"

Chief Williams heard this and came running up the street. "St. Paul's, you say?" he called up to them.

St. Paul's, at the corner of Clinton and Matthew, was a Chicago landmark on the river. If the steeple caught fire, what was to stop the flames from spreading across the river to the businesses on the other side?

"Yes, the steeple's on fire!" one of the Fiends shouted.

Chief Williams ran back down the street, shouting orders. "Lads! Get over to St. Paul's. Put up your highest ladder and get a stream engine down there!"

But I had my own job to do. I needed to get

back to the horses. The horses would need me.

I fought my way through the mob. One man had rolled a keg of beer out of a saloon into the middle of the street. He was serving free drinks, and many were partaking. Others were running into abandoned shops and coming away with their arms full of stolen goods. All of a sudden, it was open season for looters!

There you are! said Daisy when she caught sight of me.

What word? Maisy called out.

I was just getting ready to give them the grim news about St. Paul's when Maybelle's eyes widened. A shrill whinny burst from her. *Look out behind you, Sparky!*

Someone took a strong grip on my collar. I looked up to see a man with drink on his breath, and fingers like sausages. I recognized him. He was one of the looters. Before I could struggle free, he tied a rope to my collar.

I snarled and sprang.

He jerked the rope and laughed. "Fierce little thing, aren't you?"

Over his shoulder, he hoisted a tablecloth filled with loot. "I've always wanted me my own little fire doggie!" he said. "Come along, Spotty! Let's see what other goodies this fine city has to offer."

The looter dragged me down the street. What would become of my horses? What would become of me? I found myself powerless, having no choice but to run behind him or be choked by the rope.

All was chaos. A woman with her skirt on fire ran screaming past us. Another stood on the sidewalk next to a piano. We passed spectators and fugitives, beer swillers and looters, policemen and firemen, stray dogs and stampeding horses. Piles of household goods littered the streets. Some people had abandoned their belongings. Others had gone off in search of wagons to carry them away. Up ahead stood a wooden handcart halfway filled with silver and china.

"A choice array!" the looter cried, and emptied his bundle into the wagon. Tying my rope to one handle, he wheeled someone else's cart away.

Each time the looter left the cart to run into a store or home, I struggled to free myself. But the knot was too tight. I barked for help. But everyone was too busy to notice a dognapped Dal.

The more stops he made, the heavier the cart got. By the time we arrived at St. Paul's, he was winded and stopped to rest.

The crew of the *Long John* was fighting the fire in the church. I spied Chief Williams. But he looked past me to the nearby hose man.

"The fire has jumped the river!" the hose man said.

"The devil it has!" said Williams. "Go for it! I'll be there as soon as I'm able."

"Did you hear that, Spotty?" the looter said to me. "The fire's spread across the river. There are big department stores over there, hotels, and fancy homes with excellent pickings."

Moments later, we heard a tremendous crash and people screaming for help. The roof of St. Paul's had collapsed.

We continued onward, passing through poorer neighborhoods. People ran screaming from their burning shanties. Sparks and firebrands—sticks of flaming wood—borne by high winds streaked over the river as we crossed on the bridge. Anything the firebrands struck burst into flames.

Traffic on the bridges all up and down the river was heavy. Fire Fiends who had crossed to watch the fire on the other side now came streaming back to try to save their homes.

Someone shouted, "Run for your lives! The gasworks has caught fire. It's about to blow!"

Just as we made it to the other side of the bridge, an explosion rocked us.

"Was that the gasworks?" someone asked.

"No—it was gunpowder in the armory!" another shouted.

Farther on, we passed the Merchants' Union Express Building. Chief Williams was there, directing the boys from the *Long John*. They were fighting the fire working its way up the building's wooden face. A fireman ran up and shouted to Williams, "Fifth Avenue's on fire between Monroe and Madison."

Williams took off at a run. The man couldn't be everywhere at once, but tonight it certainly seemed as if he was trying.

By then I had stopped struggling to escape. I dragged along behind my captor, a beaten dog with lowered head and even lower spirits. At some point, I lifted my nose and took a look around. I was surprised to find myself standing on a street filled with grand houses. The frantic crowds had vanished. It was eerily quiet. The folks who lived here must have all fled before the fire.

This was delightfully good news for the looter, who laughed and danced as he ran into one mansion after another and helped himself to whatever had been left behind. He was searching a coach house for a bigger wagon to hold his ill-gotten goods when, suddenly, a warm hand cupped the top of my head.

A sweet voice whispered, "Why, Sparky! Is that you? What are you doing all the way over here?"

Her clothes were torn and sooty, and her face was streaked with tears, but I knew this girl. I wagged my tail and yelped with happiness at the sight of Lizzy Ryan.

"Why are you tied to this cart?" she asked. "I'm lost. My mum and the others were on their way to Uncle Finn's farm when a burning building collapsed. The horse spooked and the wagon swerved. It hit a bump. I must have fallen out and knocked my head. By the time I came to my senses, the wagon was gone. I've been running from the fire since then. Now that I've found you, I know everything will be fine."

The looter came out of the carriage house, waving his arms and hollering, "Get away from that dog! He's mine!"

"*He* is a *she,* and she belongs to the Maxwell Street fire station," Lizzy said boldly.

He raised a fist. I growled and strained against the rope. If that man laid one hand on her, so help me . . . But he pulled back and said, "Run along, girlie, and mind your own beeswax."

Scowling, Lizzy turned and flounced off down the street. I followed her with longing eyes.

The looter continued working his way down the block. "The sky's the limit, eh, Spotty?"

Grrrrrr. *If you call me Spotty one more time, I'm going to bite your tongue off.*

He had disappeared into yet another coach house, when who should come sneaking out of the bushes but Lizzy!

With one eye on the coach house door, she picked at the knot. "I can't seem to loosen it," she said.

Then, clever girl that she was, she unbuckled my collar and slipped it from my neck.

I was free!

The two of us took off running and never looked back.

ON THE RUN

Finally, Lizzy and I paused to catch our breath.

"Sorry you lost your collar, girl," she said, "but at least we're rid of that horrid man!"

I sat on my haunches and looked up at her, panting.

"We can't go back to my house. It's all gone," she said. "And there'll be no one at the station. We'll head to Uncle Finn's farm. That's where my mother and brothers are. They must be out of their minds with worry about me. Downers Grove is west. That's where we need to go."

The word *west* drew me up sharp. West was where the fire was. Were we going back into the fire? But Lizzy was in charge now, so my place was at her side.

Soon, we were struggling against the crowds pushing and shoving their way across the State Street Bridge. On the river, sailors escaped their burning ships by diving into the water. Just as we made it to the other side, I felt a sudden searing heat at my back. I whipped around.

The bridge burst into flame! Lizzy fell to her knees and buried her face in my neck. Catching our breath, we looked up at the same time as the bridge crumbled into the river.

"Oh, Sparky—that was so close!" she gasped.

We forged onward. The fire on this side of the

river was everywhere. Like a ravenous beast, it rampaged all around us. It rose up in twisting columns that exploded in the sky. It blinded us with hailstorms of embers and ash.

And the wind? Scorching hot, it reached down my throat and seemed to suck the air from my chest. It buffeted about poor Lizzy without mercy. She grabbed the scruff of my neck and held fast as if I, alone, could keep her anchored to the earth.

Roofs were ripped off houses, scattering furniture helter-skelter. I pulled Lizzy this way and that, dodging flaming mattresses and sofas and chairs as they came hurtling at us. And the noise! The roaring fire, the shrieking wind, the exploding buildings, the screaming people. I howled from the pain in my ears.

In the midst of the madness, Lizzy managed to take off her dress sash. She tied one end around her wrist and fastened the other around my neck.

She shouted at me above the din, "Now we won't get separated!"

I looked up at her and whimpered.

A man stopped and said, "Little girl, do you need help?"

"No thank you," she said politely. "I'm a Smoke-Eater's daughter, and this is a trained fire dog. We can take care of ourselves."

The man stumbled off, shaking his head.

Firemen and their equipment were everywhere. I kept hoping that one of them would recognize Lizzy. But none did.

When a burning wall started to buckle and collapse, I yelped a warning and yanked her away. We huddled behind a stone wall as a torrent of ash and cinders rained down upon us.

After a while, we found ourselves in the courthouse square, where we paused to rest near a hose truck. Fire had gutted the building. We watched as the cupola crumbled and the giant bell, which had alerted the city to so many thousands of fires, came crashing to the earth with a clang that made me bay like a hound at the full moon.

The hose man next to us removed his hat and held it over his heart. "The body of President Lincoln lay in state here. That bell rang to call the people of Chicago to national mourning. We'll never hear it ring again."

He turned to look at us with bloodshot eyes. "What are you doing, all by yourself? Where are your folks?"

"My father's fighting the fire. My mother's gone west to Downers Grove," she said. "That's where we're headed now."

"You'll never make it. There's nothing west of

here but fire and ruination. You must go northeast to Lincoln Park."

But Lizzy was sticking to her plan. As we turned to leave, the hose man's voice rang in our ears, "Hey, girlie! You're heading the wrong way!"

Wrong way or not, we kept on going. Soon we found ourselves in what Mike, on our runs through the city, called the shopping district. Chicago was a world-famous home to big department stores. We passed them as we made our way west, all of them burned to the ground. Looters swarmed everywhere, helping themselves to anything the fire hadn't claimed.

We also saw the charred remains of the city's grand hotels. In a voice made scratchy from smoke, Lizzy spoke their names as we walked: the Sherman House, the Palmer House, the Tremont, the Briggs House, and the Grand Pacific. The great theaters

had not been spared the fire's wrath, either, including the brand-new Crosby's Opera House.

The farther west we went, the more worried I became. Everyone else was going east! Could all these people be wrong?

We began to notice that the steam engines we walked past had stopped pumping. The firemen stood around and shook their heads in dismay.

Lizzy tugged on the sleeve of one of them. "Excuse me, mister, but why aren't you spraying the fire?"

The fireman said, "The waterworks went up in flames, little girl. The system stopped working."

Lizzy turned to me. For the first time, I saw doubt darken her eyes. "If the firemen have given up, the city's in real trouble, Sparky. Without water, all is lost."

We staggered onward. Lizzy's feet were dragging now. The fire had burned holes in her shoes, and her blackened toes stuck out. Her lips were cracked and dry. My paw pads were burned, but I, at least, could dip my muzzle into the grimy overflow from the hoses running in the gutters. There wasn't a drop of clean water for Lizzy.

We passed more and more firemen, just sitting around. Others lay fast asleep. I hoped that we might come upon Lizzy's father. But I could not imagine Michael Ryan sitting or sleeping while the fire burned on. Wherever he was, he was still fighting the fire any way he could, as were Sully and Joe and Jack and Mack.

But what of the horses? And the greenhorn Cinders? I could not imagine how horrific this must be for her. Had she and the others broken away?

Were they galloping loose through the streets?

Beside me, Lizzy tripped and staggered.

A wagon creaked past us.

Lizzy looked up. "That's Henry! I know that horse!" she croaked.

The horse drew to a halt at the sound of a familiar voice.

She staggered around to the side of the wagon and said to the man holding the reins, "Mr. Harkness, could you please spare me and my dog a sip of water?"

The man peered down at her. "As I live and breathe—Lizzy Ryan! Dear child, what in heaven's name are you doing in the middle of this nightmare?"

"Mr. Harkness . . . ," Lizzy said faintly. Her eyelids fluttered. He jumped down and caught her just before she fainted.

Unfastening the sash from around Lizzy's wrist, Mr. Harkness lifted her up onto the wagon seat.

I leaped into the back of the wagon, which was piled high with books. Mr. Harkness held a canteen to Lizzy's lips. Soon, she revived like a flower in a cloudburst. She sat up and looked around.

"Sparky!" she cried.

I barked and wormed my way through the books to the front seat. *Here I am!*

Lizzy stroked my head. "Mr. Harkness, this is Sparky. She's the fire dog from Father's station. I rescued her from a dognapper. She's saved my life so many times I've lost count!"

I looked away modestly. It was no more than any Dal would do.

"Sparky," Lizzy said, picking the cinders from my coat, "Mr. Harkness lives across the street from my family. He has a big library full of books."

Lizzy told Mr. Harkness how she had fallen off the wagon and gotten separated from her family and then lost. "We're on our way to join them at Uncle Finn's farm in Downers Grove."

"Then it's a good thing we met, because that's as foolish a notion as I've ever heard. No, lass.

You're coming with me. I'll keep you safe until I can get you back to your poor dear ma."

It was late Monday night when we got to Lincoln Park. It was crowded with people. They huddled on the grass and along the pebbled shoreline of Lake Michigan. But not even here were we safe from the fire. At our backs, the city burned, hotter and brighter than ever. And the wind kept sweeping the flames toward us.

Lincoln Park, where Mike and I used to run on hot summer days, stood next to an old graveyard. Although most of the graves had been moved to another cemetery, some of the old wooden grave markers had caught fire. Abandoned stone vaults had cracked open from the heat. In spots, the dry grass had burst into flame. Some people were even huddling in the open graves to shelter from the fire.

Mr. Harkness drove his wagon through the crowds and right into the lake. He didn't stop until the water came up to the top of the wheels. He dropped the reins. "There now. I dare the fire to come get us here."

Many people had the same idea. Those without wagons waded in and stood in water up to their chins. Farther out, many others bobbed around in boats or on makeshift rafts.

Lizzy wrapped her arms around me. With a relieved sigh, she dropped off to sleep. Dog-tired myself, I, too, surrendered to sleep. But I woke up suddenly when a new smell wafted my way.

It was cold and clean and smelled nothing at all like fire or smoke. I lifted my nose and twitched my nostrils.

It was the wind. It had shifted!

The next moment, a big drop of cold water hit me in the eye.

More drops began to fall, pebbling the surface of the lake.

We were saved!

10

HELP FROM ON HIGH

I leaped up and danced and barked for all the world as if the fire bell were about to ring.

On the shore, people fell to the ground and prayed their thanks. They danced in the rain and splashed in puddles. As the rain continued to fall in a steady drizzle, all eyes turned toward the city. We watched as the rain did what no amount of firemen and their equipment had been able to accomplish. It began to douse the flames.

Lizzy and I were soon soaked and shivering. Mr. Harkness found a dry blanket and bundled us up. Throughout the long night, Lizzy and I huddled together.

We awoke at sunrise. Lizzy threw off the blanket. We looked around.

It had stopped raining. In the city, small fires continued to burn, but the rain had smothered the worst of it.

People began to creep forth to see what was left. Mr. Harkness drove the wagon out of the park and headed southwest. The fire had spared the pine block road here, and it was crowded with people.

The wooden structures were reduced to ashes. Stone buildings were gutted, their limestone walls cracked or crumbled. A few lone chimneys stood in the rubble. Rarely were four walls left standing.

Through the wreckage, we rode in silence.

Mr. Harkness shook his head and wondered, "Will the city ever recover?"

But something was happening, even as we rode along. The wandering people began to stop and talk. They poked around, searching in the rubble and helping one another pull undamaged items free of the wreckage. Fishing out bricks, they stacked them up in piles.

"Well, what do you know?" said Mr. Harkness. "I guess you can't keep Chicago down for long, after all."

We passed wagons bearing loads of fresh lumber. The air rang with the sound of hammers pounding as people built temporary housing.

Chicago was already rising from the ashes.

When we got to Maxwell Street, the first person I saw was Michael Ryan standing in the entrance of the fire station, looking weary and solemn, speaking with Joe. Mr. Harkness drew up, and Lizzy jumped down.

"Daddy!" she cried.

Michael turned and looked in disbelief, tears filling his eyes.

She ran and leaped into his arms.

"Is it really you?" he cried. "Your ma sent word that you'd gone missing! We've been out of our minds with worry, we have."

"I fell out of the wagon and got lost, but then Sparky and I found each other. We've been through so much together," she said.

Looking toward the wagon, Michael said, "Chief?"

I jumped down and ran to him.

"Is that my Sparky dog beneath all that soot?"

I barked and danced for joy.

"And here we were fretting that the fire had

claimed your spotted self," said Michael.

"It wasn't the fire," said Lizzy. "It was a looter. He dognapped Sparky. I found her way over on the north side, where I'd fled from the fire. We helped each other."

Michael knelt down and rubbed me roughly until the soot came off me in black clouds. "And to think that all this time you were looking after my Lizzy."

"Sparky's the best dog in the world," Lizzy said.

"Well, of course she is," said Michael. "She's a hero. With a hero's raging thirst, too, I'll bet."

Michael set down a bowl of water and they all watched me lap it up thirstily. Afterward, I went to check on the others.

The boys were scrubbing the Thoroughbreds with rainwater and soapsuds and brushing the ashes out of their teeth.

You missed all the excitement, said Maisy. The whites of her eyes were bloodred.

We'd given you up for lost, said Daisy. Her tail had burned down to the stub.

We were fixing to mourn you, said Maybelle.

Mum had limped down the stairs. *Aren't you a sight for sore eyes,* she said.

I looked around for Cinders and saw her with her head down in a big pile of hay. Her legs were wrapped in bandages.

How did Cinders fare? I asked.

Not bad, said Daisy.

Very well, in fact, said Maisy.

For a greenhorn, Maybelle added.

Cinders raised her head. I went and touched the tip of my cold black nose to the velveteen warmth of hers.

I'm proud of you, Cindy, I said.

Cinders blew out, then went back to her hay.

They say the fire is giving Chicago a fresh start, I
said to her. *And I guess the same is true for you.*

And what about me? a raspy voice called out.

A shuffling sound came from one of the open stalls. Then out limped the last character on earth I expected to see—the Little Lion himself.

Khan, the long-lost chow chow!

His puffy red coat was burned in patches, but there was no mistaking him.

At first, my back went up. What was this tosser doing on my turf?

Then Michael put a hand on my head. "Easy, Chief. That scruffy fuzz ball showed up to do your job when you went missing. He turned out to be a good little volunteer fire dog, he did."

Michael's right, said Cinders. *This noble beast saw me through the worst of the fire.*

I went over and sniffed at Khan. *You smell worse than a burning dump pile.*

You don't exactly smell like a rose yourself, said Khan, sniffing me back.

Six months—and several baths—later, I whelped my first litter of pups beneath the stairs of the

Maxwell Street station. There were nine of them. Some had spots. Some had furry ruffs. Some had tongues as black as licorice. Others were all three rolled into one. They were all as dear to me as their sire, my fine mate, Khan.

Firemen from all over Chicago lined up for a chance to adopt our pups. And, as you might expect, every single one grew up to be a first-rate Smoke-Eater.

APPENDIX

The Great Chicago Fire

In 1871, Chicago was the fourth-largest city in America. Located on the western shores of Lake Michigan, it boasted a population of 334,000. The wealthier people lived in mansions in the city's southeast district. Poorer folks lived scattered about in shacks and tenements in the west, north, and south. The business district, located in the center of the city, included office buildings, department stores, theaters, opera houses, and grand hotels. Along the two branches of the Chicago River, which ran through the city, there were wharves, lumberyards, workshops, warehouses, coal yards, and bridges. Wood, sourced from the great forests to the north, was the primary building material.

Even buildings made of stone were covered with wooden decorations. Wooden sidewalks raised pedestrians above the mud. Of the 538 miles of streets, only 88 miles were paved, and 57 of those were paved with wooden blocks. All in all, Chicago was a highly flammable city.

In the late 1800s, most towns and cities in America still had volunteer fire departments. But Chicago boasted 25 fire departments manned by 185 paid, trained professional firefighters. These firefighters were headed up by district commissioners who were, in turn, managed by a chief commissioner. These men had their work cut out for them. In 1868 alone, 515 fires were recorded in the city, an average of two alarms every day. A central watchman, located in the tower of the courthouse, kept an eye out for fires. In addition, each fire station had a watchman. When the courthouse watchman spotted a fire, he rang the bell and telegraphed the fire stations nearest to the blaze. If someone on the street spotted flames, they went to the nearest firebox to alert the courthouse, which notified the proper fire station. The giant courthouse bell tolled a code that broadcasted the fire's location. There were also special insurance patrols, men who patrolled the streets on foot, ready to put out small fires with extinguishers or turn in alarms for bigger blazes. Chicago, in short, was a city braced for fire. So you might well ask, if Chicago was so well prepared, how did a small fire in a dairy barn result in a citywide disaster like the Great Fire?

The afternoon of Sunday, October 8, 1871, was unseasonably warm and dry. The summer-long drought had lasted into the fall. The trees drooped with dry leaves, and a steady wind from the southwest gusted and swirled. Just the day before, a sixteen-hour blaze had exhausted the city's firefighters and taxed their equipment, including most of the city's seventeen steam engines.

We will never know for sure what started the fire, but we do know where it started: in Mrs. O'Leary's dairy barn, on the corner of DeKoven and Jefferson Streets. Legend has it that one of her cows kicked over a kerosene lantern. There was even a famous song written about it:

One dark night, when people were in bed,
Mrs. O'Leary lit a lantern in her shed,
The cow kicked it over, winked its eye, and said,
There'll be a hot time in the old town tonight.

Later, an official investigation revealed that the cow was probably not to blame, nor was

Mrs. O'Leary, who had gone to bed early that night. Perhaps the story of the guilty cow survives in popular myth and imagination because it was such a simple explanation. But the real cause of the fire remains murky. One theory has it that guests of the O'Learys' tenants—who were having a party—went to the barn to get milk and accidentally kicked over the lantern. Another theory maintains that boys smoking and playing poker in the hayloft started it. Still another attributes the fire to a falling meteor! We do know that a friend of the O'Learys', Daniel "Peg Leg" Sullivan, testified that he called on the family at nine o'clock and discovered that they had all gone to bed. Sullivan had sat down to rest his stump when he spotted smoke. "Pat! Kate!" he shouted. "Your barn is on fire!"

There was a firebox on the nearby corner, at Goll's Drugstore. Mr. Goll later said he sent in two alarms. But watchers at the courthouse claimed never to have received them. Was the firebox not working properly, or was Mr. Goll lying? We'll never know. But we do know that the courthouse watchers incorrectly pegged the location of the fire and repeatedly sounded the wrong alarms. Only two fire companies whose lookouts had spotted flames—Engine Company 6 (*Little Giant*), located on Maxwell Street, and Engine Company 5 (*U.P. Harris*), located on West Jackson Street—arrived right away. All the others went on a wild-goose chase, giving the fire a head start.

Within the first hour, the wind drove the fire into neighboring yards. Barns, houses, chicken coops, trees, sidewalks, and fences went up in flames. Neighbors helped residents pull furniture, clothes, and family members to safety while the flames leaped from roof to roof.

Commissioner Robert A. Williams, the city-wide head of the fire department, arrived to supervise. He ordered the men to surround the fire. But the fire jumped over their heads and fanned out. The wind whipped up the flames, causing a phenomenon known as a fire devil. As heated air rose and met cooler air, it began to spin like a tornado. The fire "devils" whirled, carrying sparks, burning firebrands, and debris, spreading the conflagration far and wide.

The fire advanced, unchecked. Embers fell, according to eyewitnesses, like "a blizzard of red snow." Some of them landed on St. Paul's Church, four blocks away from the O'Learys' barn. The steeple caught fire, and from there, the embers blew across the river into the business district and wealthy residential district. As the fire made its way through the city, it burned down shantytowns as well as mansions. It destroyed factories and businesses, hotels and department stores, theaters and bridges and office buildings. When the city waterworks burned down at three o'clock on Monday morning, the fire pumps stopped being able to draw water.

As Monday morning dawned, the mayor sent out an SOS: "Chicago in flames." Help soon came pouring in from Milwaukee, Cincinnati, Dayton, Louisville, Detroit, Pittsburgh, and other cities. Despite all the efforts, the fire continued to run rampant. The streets were mobbed with looters, people fleeing the fire, and spectators watching in horrified fascination.

Thirty thousand homeless people flocked to Lincoln Park, on the shores of Lake Michigan. The fire burned all of Monday and well into the night. It might well have gone on burning, too, were it not for the rain that started falling late that night. The showers slowed down the spread long enough for firefighters to get the upper hand.

By the time the fire was out, it had destroyed an area four miles long and a mile wide, burning 18,000 buildings and 73 miles of street. It killed 300 people and left another 100,000 homeless. Newspaper writers called it the Great Fire.

It would be nice to think that the Great Fire brought about a much-needed revolution in city building codes and practices. But Chicago was in such a hurry to rebuild after the fire that it did so thoughtlessly and largely with wood. It wasn't until after the Little Fire three years later that a reformation came about. The Chicago that stands today— known for its beautifully designed stone buildings, broad concrete sidewalks, and wide boulevards— is largely the result of this second fire. Still, it is the Great Fire of 1871 that stands out in memory. Today, the Chicago Fire Academy, where new firefighters train, stands on the corner of DeKoven and Jefferson Streets. A spot marked on the floor claims to be the exact location where Mrs. O'Leary's barn caught fire.

Want to know more about the Great Chicago Fire? Go to chicagohs.org.

Did Mrs. O'Leary's cow really start the fire? Visit this site to read an in-depth investigation: greatchicagofire.org.

About the Dalmatian

While Yugoslavia has an area called Dalmatia, there is no evidence that the breed either originated from this region or was named for it. Since ancient times, spotted dogs have been seen all over Europe and North Africa. They can be seen painted on the walls of Egyptian tombs and in frescoes at the Dominican Catholic Church of Santa Maria Novella in Italy, built in 1360. The symbol of the Dominican religious order was a black-and-white dog, perhaps because the priests wore white habits with black capes. The costume was known as the dalmatic. More elaborate dalmatics were made of white ermine with bits of black tails sewn into it. Did the garment give the breed its name, or was it the other way around? No one knows for sure.

Built for speed and endurance, Dalmatians have served as sporting dogs, war dogs, shepherds, ratters, and coach dogs. But they are best known in America as fire dogs. Before there were fire trucks, firemen carried their equipment in wheeled rigs. At first, they hauled the rigs themselves. Then they got the smart idea to have horses pull the rigs for them.

A fire dog's job was to run alongside the fire horses, helping them to stay on course and not spook, either on the way to the fire or once they were on-site. Fires are noisy and scary places, and horses are high-strung. There was something about the Dalmatians that kept the horses calm and steady. In the years since motorized trucks have replaced horses, firefighters still keep Dalmatians as house mascots, in memory of how it was in the old days.

A medium-sized, muscular dog, the Dalmatian stands nineteen to twenty-three inches at the shoulder and weighs forty-eight to fifty-five pounds. It is the only breed that is truly spotted. The spots are black or liver (dark brown) against a white coat. A Dalmatian is born all white and gets its spots at three weeks of age. By one year, it will have gotten most of its spots, but more can show up in later years.

For more information on this distinctive breed, visit akc.org/dog-breeds/dalmatian.

Owning a Dalmatian

The Dalmatian is a strong, active, alert, and highly intelligent dog. It makes a great family pet as well as a watchdog. But like all watchdogs, it can be shy or aggressive with strangers. With its short hair, it is easy to groom but does shed year-round, so you'll have fine white hairs all over your clothes and furniture. Like any active breed, the Dalmatian needs plenty of exercise to stay happy and healthy.

A certain popular animated movie and television series created a high demand for Dalmatians, which led irresponsible breeders to get in on the act. If you think a Dalmatian is the right dog for you, make sure you go to a reputable breeder or a rescue organization.

For more information on the Dalmatian as a possible pet, go to thedca.org.

A Word About Chow Chows

One of the most ancient dog breeds in existence, the chow chow dates back two thousand years to northern China, where it was probably the result of crossing the Samoyed with the Tibetan mastiff. Its Chinese name, *Songshi Quan,* means "puffy lion dog," and it is believed to be the model for the Foo dog statues that guard Buddhist temples and palaces. According to legend, it got its black tongue from licking the color from the sky on the day of Creation. Queen Victoria owned some chow chows that were said to have inspired the look of the very first commercial teddy bear. With its lion's mane ruff, its deep-set almond eyes, and its stiff-legged gait, the chow chow has a noble, even snobbish, look. Some say it has a streak of stubbornness. But like all dogs, given early socialization and proper training, the chow chow makes a loyal pet and a worthy companion.

For more information on the chow chow, go to chowclub.org/ccci.

CORNER
STATE & MADISON ST
AFTER CHICAGO FIRE

View of the destruction shortly after the fire

Fire Dogs from 1910 to 2016

Get the horse's side of the story.

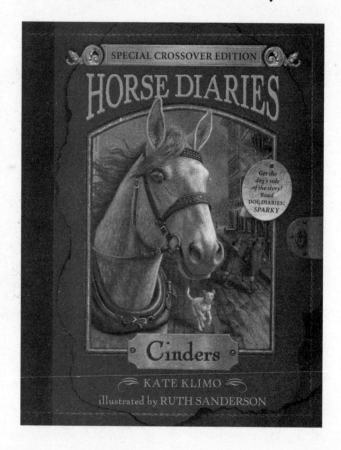

SPECIAL CROSSOVER EDITION

HORSE DIARIES

Get the dog's side of the story! Read DOG DIARIES: SPARKY

Cinders

KATE KLIMO

illustrated by RUTH SANDERSON